Anonymous

Legends of Our Lady and the Saints

Our Children's Book of Stories in verse. Part 1

Anonymous

Legends of Our Lady and the Saints
Our Children's Book of Stories in verse. Part 1

ISBN/EAN: 9783337300173

Printed in Europe, USA, Canada, Australia, Japan

Cover: Foto ©Andreas Hilbeck / pixelio.de

More available books at **www.hansebooks.com**

LEGENDS

OF

OUR LADY AND THE SAINTS;

OR,

OUR CHILDREN'S BOOK OF STORIES,
IN VERSE,

WRITTEN FOR THE RECITATIONS OF THE PUPILS OF THE
SCHOOLS OF THE HOLY CHILD JESUS,

ST. LEONARDS-ON-SEA.

PART I.

LONDON: BURNS, OATES, & CO.,

17 AND 18 PORTMAN STREET, W., AND 63 PATERNOSTER ROW, E.C.

1870.

ST. LEONARDS-ON-SEA :

PRINTED AT THE CONVENT OF THE HOLY CHILD JESUS.

These Legends,

told in Simple Verse, are

Dedicated

to all our Dear Children of the

Schools of the Holy Child Jesus,

that by them

their Confidence in the Power of

Mary and the Saints

may increase, and mingling with the memories

of the lessons of their early days, learnt

in the House of the Holy Child,

may lead them

to Know, Love, and Serve Him, who is

"Glorious in His Saints,

Wonderful in His Majesty, doing Wonders."

St. Leonards-on-Sea,
July 7th, 1870.

INDEX.

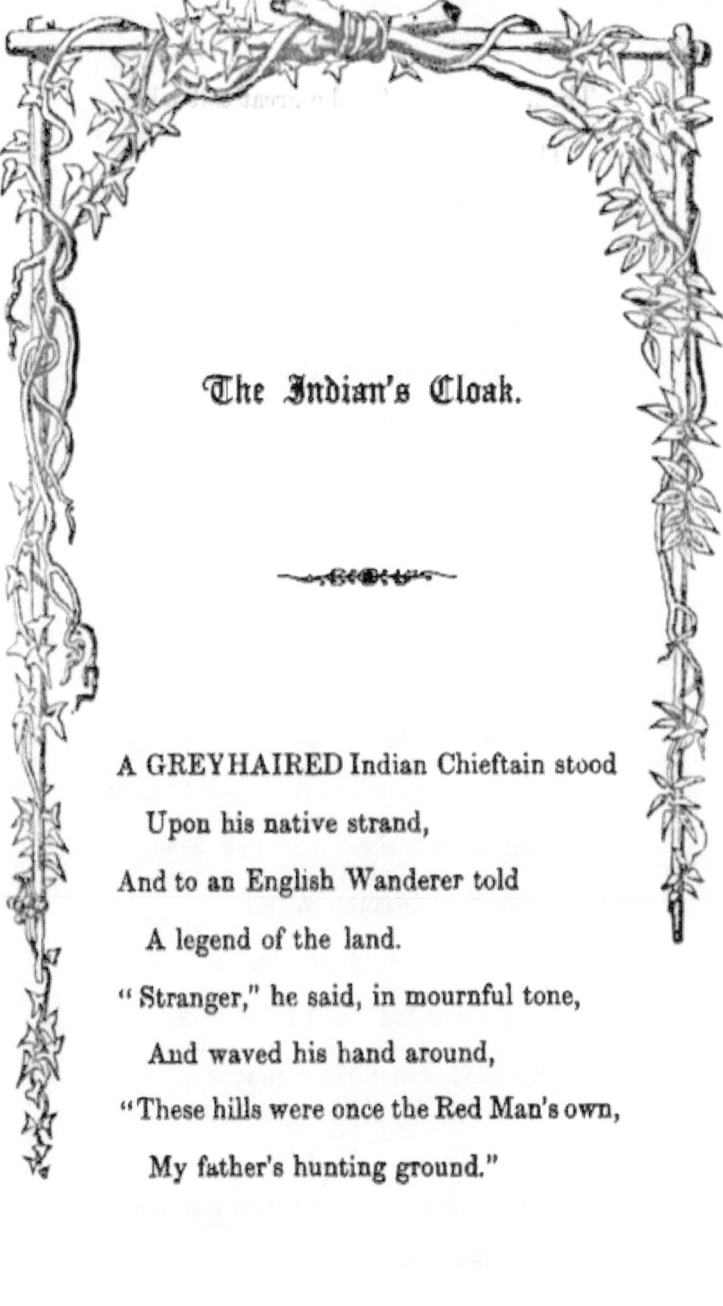

The Indian's Cloak.

A GREYHAIRED Indian Chieftain stood
  Upon his native strand,
And to an English Wanderer told
  A legend of the land.
" Stranger," he said, in mournful tone,
  And waved his hand around,
"These hills were once the Red Man's own,
  My father's hunting ground."

II.

Then, stranger, o'er the great salt lake
   The pale face warriors came,
There was no mercy in their hearts,
   They spoke with tongues of flame ;
They drove the red man o'er the hills
   Like hunted deer away,
Till in the land our fathers ruled
   Scarce one was found to stray.

III.

The hunter's village rose no more
   Upon the hill-side green,
Their footsteps might not tread the shore
   Which once their own had been.
To the great Manitou aloud
   They cried in their despair,
His face was hid behind a cloud,
   He heeded not their prayer.

IV.

" 'Twas then the black-robed Fathers came,
   The forest paths they trod,

They spoke of Blessed Mary's name,
    And of the white man's God,
They led the hunters back once more,
    The wigwams rose again,
They made our fathers till the ground,
    And live like Christian men.

V.

There was a mighty chieftain's son,
    The noblest of his race,
And here, upon Quantitlan's plain,
    He made his dwelling place.
He knew each tale of Mary dear,
    The black-robed Fathers tell,
The hunter's heart was warm and true,
    He loved our Lady well.

VI.

And as each seventh sun came round,
    He o'er the plain would pass,
. And seek the pale face city proud
    To hear our Lady's Mass.

C*

My brother, high on yonder hill,
   A holy Church may see,
" Twas there he ever paused to sing
   Her hymns and Litany."

VII.

No Christian Church was standing there,
   The hill was smooth and green,
But there, he knew, in ancient days
   A heathen grove had been.
And much he wished to drive away,
   By holy song and prayer,
And, by the white Christ's Mother's name,
   The demons lurking there.

VIII.

Once, as he sang in Mary's praise,
   Upon that spot, alone,
He heard a sweet and wondrous strain
   That mingled with his own.
He deemed right well no earthly voice
   Such heavenly song could frame,

When lo! from out a brilliant cloud
    Was gently breathed his name.

IX.

Pale face! the summer sunset clouds
    Are floods of glory bright,
But they are pale and cold compared
    With the fair dream of light
That then the wandering chieftain saw
    Upon yon hill-side green!
A Lady robed in dazzling white,
    He knew the Angels' Queen.

X.

" I know thy love, my child," she said,
    " And I will have thee raise
Upon the spot where now I stand
    A Church in Mary's praise.
Seek thou the black-robed Chief of prayer,
    And speak these words from me,
None shall invoke their Mother here
    Whose prayer unheard shall be."

XI.

The Indian sped upon his way,
  He sought the Chief of prayer,
He told how he had seen that day
  The white Christ's Mother fair.
The father's face was cold and grave,
  He would not truth receive,
" It is a wondrous tale," he said,
  " But I may not believe."

XII.

Again the chieftain passed the hill,
  Again that light he saw,
Again that voice his spirit filled,
  With faith and love and awe.
" Hast thou performed my will, my child ?"
  Were the sweet sounds he heard ;
" Lady, the Black-robe heedeth not
  An Indian hunter's word."

XIII.

" Seek thou the black-robed Chief again,
  Once more repeat my will,

I charge him by his love to me
  My bidding to fulfil;
Go, thou, to-morrow." And he went,
  The Father only smiled,
"Thine errand thou hast done," he said,
  "Go then, in peace, my child."

XIV.

Sadly he took his homeward way,
  There Mary stood once more,
" And hast thou better sped to-day
  Than thou hast done before?"
" The black-robed Chief will not believe."
  " That is no fault of thine,
Return to-morrow, thou shalt bear
  To him, from me, a sign."

XV.

Again he came—our Lady smiled,
  A gentle sign she made,
"On yonder hill are flowers, my child,
  Bring them to me," she said.

The fragrance of the blushing rose
  Was borne upon the air,
Pale Face! it was the moon of snows,
  Yet flowers were blooming there!

XVI.

Lilies and roses in a wreath
  Bid Mary's fingers twine,
"Go, bear it to the black-robed Chief,
  For this shall be my sign."
Within his woollen mantle rough
  The perfumed treasure lay,
And once again the Indian trod
  The city's crowded way.

XVII.

One drew the hunter's robe aside,
  And saw the garland fair,
He knew no earthly bower supplied
  Those blossoms rich and rare ;
The Black-robe listened to the tale,
  And came in haste to see,

"And hath Our Lady sent a sign,"
  He, said, "my son to me"?

XVIII.

The chieftain opened wide his cloak,
  When lo! no flowers were there!
But drawn as though by Angels hand
  Our Lady's image fair.
The black-robed Father bent his knee
  In reverence to the ground,
And soon that wondrous sign to see
  Came thousands flocking round.

XIX.

Upon the hill where Mary stood
  Yon holy church was raised,
And flashing bright with gems and gold
  Our Lady's Altar blazed.
Princes and chiefs to deck her shrine
  With earth's rare gifts have striven,
But oh, the costliest treasure there
  By Mary's self was given.

These few lines were written on the "Legend of our Lady of Guadaloupe." The story is in brief as follows: A poor Indian, who had a great devotion to the holy Mother of God, was in the habit, whenever he passed a certain hill where a heathen temple had once stood, of singing the Litany of Loretto with the pious intention of putting to flight any evil spirits who might yet linger there.

On one occasion our dear Lady appeared to him, and commanded her pious servant to go to the Bishop of Mexico, and declare it to be her will that a church should be erected in her honour on that very spot. The vision was repeated three times, but still the Bishop refused to give credence to a tale which bore little appearance of probability. But when for the third time the Indian recounted the failure of his mission to the Blessed Virgin, she told him to mount to the summit of the hill, and bring her from thence some flowers which he would find blooming there. The hunter obeyed, and returned bearing in his hand some rich blossoms which Mary entwined into a garland, telling him to carry it to the Bishop in token of the truth of his statement.

The Indian received the precious wreath, carefully laid it in his cloak and carried it to Mexico, where, on unfolding it at the feet of the Bishop he found, not a half-faded wreath, but a beautiful representation of our Lady impressed on the rough woollen cloth. A Church was forthwith erected on the hill dedicated by the Spaniards to Our Lady of Guadaloupe.

The Indian's Cloak, now regarded as a sacred relic, was suspended over the High Altar, and in process of time a famous pilgrimage was erected there.

Legend of St. Christopher.

ERE yet the Gospel had been preached
In countries that it since has reached,
In Canaan's Land, so we are told,
There dwelt a giant, strong and bold.
To no one would he homage pay,
Who held not undivided sway;
And so he journeyed far and wide,
But with no master would abide.
Wearied, at length, the court he gained
Of one, for wealth and power famed,

D

To whom no monarch could be found
Equal in might the whole earth round.
With him, then, Christopher remained,
And joyfully was entertained.
By chance, it so fell out one day,
A minstrel, passing by that way,
Came in the presence of the king,
Before the court to play and sing.
Full oft he spoke of Satan dread,
And ev'ry time the name was said
The monarch cross'd himself, and pray'd
Ne'er to be Satan's captive made.
"Who is this prince you do so fear?"
Said Christopher who then was near,
"If he be greater than thou art,
"Him will I serve, and hence depart."
With that he journeyed forth again,
And as he crossed a desert plain,
A vast assembly came in sight
Of men equipp'd, as tho' for fight.
Their chief, thus Christopher address'd ;
"Well known to me is thy behest ;

"I am the master thou dost need

"Renown'd by many a mighty deed."

With Satan, Christopher did stay,

Until at length they came one day

Nigh to a road, where four paths met,

And in the midst a Cross was set.

The demon then was forced to say

He could not pass along that way;

That Sign he was constrain'd to fly

Since Christ upon the Cross did die.

So forth went Christopher once more,

Griev'd that his search not yet was o'er,

Yet would not rest till he had found

The Lord, who thus had Satan bound.

Full many a day and night had passed

In weary toil, ere he at last

Came to an ancient hermit's cell,

Who of the long sought Christ could tell.

"But," said the man of God, "if thou

"Would'st truly find thy Lord, from now

"To fast and pray thou must begin,

"And thus thou shalt be freed from sin."

On hearing this the giant frown'd;

"To no such service I'll be bound,

"Fasting will waste my strength away,

"And I have never learnt to pray!"

"Know'st thou," the hermit then replied,

"A stream close by, both deep and wide,

"Since thou wilt neither fast nor pray,

"Beside that river thou must stay,

"And thou must use thy strength to save

"Pilgrims, who perish in the wave."

Then Christopher went forth with joy,

Well satisfied with this employ.

And never weary of his task,

None did in vain his succour ask.

Now, after many days thus spent,

One evening, as to rest he went,

He heard a voice, as of a child

Who called to him, in accents mild;

"Come Christopher, I Thee implore,

Come, bear me to the other shore."

Then going forth, he sought around,

A child was seated on the ground;

The little one of beauty rare

To Christopher renewed his prayer.

The giant raised that tiny form,

But such a burden ne'er had borne;

The waters rose, the winds they blew,

The child each moment heavier grew,

And Christopher began to think

He 'neath that mighty weight must sink.

With effort strong, he reached the shore,

And to the infant spoke once more,

"Who art thou, child, so full of grace,

"That in such peril me did place?

"To carry the whole world I deem,

"A lighter burden would have been."

Then said the child, "No marvel there,

"For in my person thou didst bear

"Him, who hath earth's foundations lain,

"To serve whom truly is to reign.

"Pleasing thy work has been to me,

"And God has shown Himself to thee."

Then Christopher believed the word,

He from that little child had heard;

And prostrate on the ground adored,

Owning the Infant for his Lord.

Sir Rodolph of Hapsbourgh.

The sunlight falls on the Alpine heights
 And jewels of every hue
Flash out from the snow-wreaths sparkling bright,
 'Neath a heaven of cloudless blue.
And the deer through the rocks on the mountain side
 Spring forward with eager bound,
While a thousand echoes ring far and wide
 To the hunter's bugle sound.

II.

Oh, well may the wild deer bound away
    Through those mountain-forests grand,
For Sir Rodolph of Hapsbourgh rides to-day
    At the head of a hunter band.
The highest places in field and hall
    Doth brave Sir Rodolph claim,
Stainless and bright is the sword he wears,
    And high is his knightly fame.

III.

Glad as a boy in the mountain chase,
    And gay as a child is he,
Yet he yieldeth to none of his noble race
    In Christian Chivalry.
And his sword that never gave heedless wound,
    Or struck at a fallen foe,
To fight for the weak from its sheath would bound,
    Or to lay the tyrant low.

IV.

His laugh rings out at the sportive jest,
    There is mirth in his dark blue eye,

His steed and his arm are fleetest and best
　　When the deer and the hounds sweep by!
But his voice in council is deep and grave
　　As the oldest and sternest there,
And the hunter gay, and the soldier brave,
　　Is meek as a child at prayer.

V.

And now · Sir Rodolph, in boyish glee
　　Rides swift as the mountain wind,
Till all his band, save a youthful page
　　Are left in the hills behind.
But he raises his bugle with joyous shout,
　　And he wends a merry blast,
Ha! Ha! good Hubert! they little thought
　　We should ride so far and fast.

VI.

They answer below;—but a softer sound
　　Comes borne on the breeze's swell,
Now, why doth the Count in such haste dismount
　　At the sound of that tinkling bell?

D*

And why is his cap doffed reverently ?

And why doth he bend the knee?

There are none, save the page, or the peasant nigh,

And the mountain lord is he !

VII.

The lord of the mountains doffed cap and plume

A nobler than he to greet,

And the chieftain of Hapsbourgh bendeth low

His Monarch and Lord to meet.

An aged priest to the plains below

Toils over the rocky road,

His hands are clasped, and his head is bowed,

For he beareth the hidden God.

VIII.

The priest hath paused beside the Count,

Sir Rodolph whispers low,

"For His dear sake who died for me

A boon thou shalt bestow !

I crave a boon for my dear Lord's sake !

And thou shalt not me deny,

My gallant steed in His service take,
  We will follow, my page and I."

IX.

"Nay, nay, Sir Knight, it must not be,
  A hunter chieftain thou—
Thine eager train e'en now I see,
  Far in the plain below."
"My train to day must ride alone,—
  Most foul disgrace 't would be,
If thou on foot shouldst bear the Lord
  Who bore the Cross for me."

X.

"And God forefend that Christain, e'er,
  Begirt with Knighthood's sword,
Should leave a mountain serf to be
  Sole follower of his Lord."
The good priest mounts the noble steed,
  Sir Rodolph holds the rein,
With careful step and reverend mien
  Thus wend they to the plain.

XI.

The dying man his God receives—
  They mount the hill once more,
And in the pass the grateful priest
  Would fain the steed restore.
"Nay, father, nay," Sir Rodolph said,
  And loosed the hunter's rein,
"The charger that hath borne my Lord,
  I may not mount again."

XII.

"A faithful servant he hath been,
  And well beloved by me,
God grant my noble steed may prove
  As true a friend to thee."
"Farewell! thy homeward path is short
  Down yonder wooded knoll,
Forget not in the Holy Mass
  To pray for my poor soul."

XIII.

A moment on his upturned face
  The priest in silence gazed,

Then solemnly his aged hands
  O'er Rodolph's head he raised.
"Sir hunter, when nine circling years
  Have passed upon their way,
Thy loving Master will reward
  Thy service of to-day."

XIV.

They passed—Fair Hapsburgh's youthful chief
  A stalwart knight had grown,
And now they need a king to fill
  His native land's proud throne!
Nor hath his manhood's fame belied
  The hope of early years,
For he is first in rank and name
  Among his gallant peers.

XV.

Now serfs and nobles bend the knee,
  To own with one accord,
As monarch of their German land,
  Fair Hapsbourgh's noble Lord,

And well the Count remembered then,
  The hoary father's words;
"Thy loyal service of to-day,
  Thy Lord will well reward."

The Christmas Rose.

'Twas near the holy Christmas time,
The snow lay thick around,
A child beside a cottage played
Upon the frozen ground.
No fire was on the cottage hearth,
The widow's home was bare,
And through the wood she shivering went
To gather firewood there.

The child gazed sadly on the stream,
Bound in its ice-chains bright,
And sadly on the brown old trees,
And on the snow wreaths white.

Poor little child! it was so cold,
Its tiny feet were blue,
And not a playmate in the world
The lonely baby knew.

The tears fell thickly from its eyes,
By hunger drawn, and pain,
And wearily it cried, "O when
Will flowers come back again?

O when will flowers come, and the sun
Shine in the clear blue sky?
I wish that I were in the land
Where roses never die."

"I have bright roses," said a voice,
"That I will give to thee,
"And I will bring the sunshine bright,
"If thou wilt play with me."

And lo! beside the cottage door
In robes of sparkling white,

Another rosy infant stood,

In childish beauty bright,—

A rosebud in his little hand

He held, and sweetly smiled:—

"See, I have brought you summer flow'rs,"

He said—dear little child.

Soft sunshine floated round his form,

His voice was low and sweet,

And fragrant flowers grew in his path,

Where'er he set his feet.

The lonely child looked up with joy,

He felt the cold no more,

He drew the stranger to his side,

Within the cottage door.

And long they sported full of glee,

Until the stranger told

Of his bright country, far away,

Beyond the clouds of gold.

"And now I must no longer stay

" But when this flower you see,--

" Unfold its petals, I will come

" And bear you home with me."

The widow sought her lonely home,
At the dark evening hour,
She heard her little one's strange tale,
And saw that wondrous flower:
But sadly on the mother's heart
Fell the babe's words of joy,
She knew full well that Stranger Child
Would come to call her boy.

The Christmas snow looks cold and bright,
But all the widow's room
Is filled with fragrance, rich and soft,
Like roses' sweet perfume.

The mystic flower hath opened wide
Its petals to the light,
But on his bed the infant lay,
A lily cold and white.

The mother wept, and wrung her hands,
When lo! a child's sweet voice
In tones of angel music said,
"O weep not, but rejoice!

"Surely this earth is cold and drear!
"I am the Christ Child bright—

"Look up, thy son is with me here,

"Radiant with heaven's own light."

The mother raised her tearful eyes,

But mortal never knew

The glory of the heavenly light

That met her raptured view.

She clasped her hands, and moved her lips,

But yet, no word they spoke,

And in that trance of joy and love

The mother's glad heart broke.

Mater Admirabilis.

When the Faith was strong in England
    Long ago, a hamlet stood
Amid green and smiling meadows,
    In the shadow of a wood.

II.

There a little shepherd maiden
    Kept her flocks from day to day,
And she learned among the meadows
    And the wood and glades to pray.

III

Poor she was, and all unlettered,
  But a yearning filled her heart,
For she longed to visit Mary
  In the shrines she loved the best.

IV.

Once, a pilgrim sought the village,
  And the orphan heard him tell
Of the house where our sweet Lady
  Had been wont on earth to dwell.

V.

Of its bands of saintly pilgrims,
  Of the costly gifts they made,
Of the wax lights and the jewels
  Round the golden shrine displayed.

VI.

And her trouble to the pilgrim
  Did the little maiden tell,
How she could not see the Mother
  She had loved so long and well.

VII

And the old Church in the valley,
　It was all too far away,
She could scarcely stay a moment,
　When she went there every day.

VIII.

Holy men are kind, like Jesus,
　So the agéd pilgrim smiled,
And he gave a little image
　Of our Lady, to the child.

IX.

And he fixed it for her firmly
　In the trunk of an old tree,
"This must be your shrine, my daughter,
　Say some Aves here for me."

X.

From that time, to deck her treasure
　Was the little maid's delight;
And the image of her mother
　Was her dream by day and night.

XI.

Gems and gold, in truth, she had not,
    But in every hedgerow green
Did the wild rose and the woodbine
    Wreathe sweet garlands for their Queen.

XII.

In the Springtide, violets purple
    Perfumed all the sunny air,
And the clematis, in Autumn,
    Hung her silver treasures there.

XIII.

Even Winter, when the snow drift
    On the earth lay cold and white,
Yielded garlands for our Lady,
    Leaves and holly berries bright.

XIV.

Friend nor parent had the maiden,
    So she raised a tiny cot,
'Neath the old oak's spreading branches,
    And she dwelt upon the spot.

XV.

There in hunger, toil, and hardship,
  Lived she lowly and unknown,
For the rich gifts of her spirit
  Could be seen by God alone.

XVI.

Till the good priest of the village
  To her hut was called one day,
For they said the shepherd maiden
  Soon from earth must pass away.

XVII.

But he paused in silent wonder,
  When he reached the cottage door,
Gazing awe-struck on a vision,
  Such as ne'er was seen before.

XVIII.

Friend nor parent had the maiden,
  Yet, there stood a lady there,
O'er the wretched pallet bending
  With a mother's tender care.

E*

XIX.

Tall she was, an azure mantle
　Wrapped her queenly form around,
And her brow of radiant beauty
　With a wreath of gems was bound.

XX.

Now she wiped the death-damps chilly,
　From the dying girl's cold brow,
And with words of tend'rest comfort,
　Kissed the patient sufferer now.

XXI.

Then she spoke aloud, and never
　Through long years of toil and care,
Did the priest forget the music
　Of those accents sweet and clear.

XXII.

"See my child! to thy poor dwelling,
　Hath thy loving Jesus come,
He will guard thy last long journey
　We shall quickly be at home."

XXIII.

Trembling, then the good priest entered,
  And he knelt beside the bed,
While the whispered last confession
  Of the dying girl was made.

XXIV.

In her arms the Lady raised her,
  While soft beams of radiant light
Filled the poor and lonely cottage
  With a glory wond'rous bright.

XXV.

While sweet strains of Angel music,
  And the mystic sounds of prayer
Told, that He, her Lord, was coming,
  To His suffering daughter there.

XXVI.

He has come! the heavenly music
  Sinks to murmurs, soft and low,
There is joy on that pale forehead,
  Earth-bound hearts can never know.

XXVII.

There is one bright look of welcome,
  For her Everlasting Guest,
And that ardent, yearning spirit
  Is for evermore at rest.

XXVIII.

When the good priest looked around him,
  He was kneeling there alone,
For the queenly form, in silence,
  From the dead girl's side had gone.

XXIX.

Still the sound of heavenly music
  In its mystic cadence rung,
And a strange unearthly fragrance
  Round the old straw pallet hung.

XXX.

While a sweet voice gently whispered
  " Sing the praises of thy Queen,
And to move men's hearts to love Her,
  Tell the vision thou hast seen.

XXXI.

"Say that none shall live unaided;
  None alone and friendless die
Who have loved Her; for a mother
  To her children must be nigh."

XXXII.

So the Father told the story
  In the lonely hamlet round,
And they built a little chapel,
On the consecrated ground.

XXXIII.

And an old oak tree within it
  Might for many a year be seen,
With an image of our Lady
  Wreathed with flowers and garland green.

The Three Flowers of The Great Mountain.

Whither away so fast, Annette,
　　Ere the morning lights the sky?
The moon in the heavens has scarcely set,
　　And the stars still shine on high.

II.

This is the feast of our village Church,
　　And I heard the pastor say
That Jesus will smile on the fairest flowers
　　Shall be laid at his feet to-day.

III.

In the farmer's garden are flowers, Annette,
  Bright roses and lilies fair;
You may go to sleep for an hour as yet,
  Then gather your garland there.

IV.

Ah, yes, bright roses are there, I know,
  And the lilies are fair to see,
But then, for the farmer's wife they grow,
  They do not bloom for me.

V.

By the meadow path there are flowers, Annette,
  White daisies and cowslips wild,
The blue-bell tall, and the violet,—
  Give them to the Holy Child.

VI.

I cannot gather my garland there,
  Though the meadow flowers are sweet,
They grow to the pathway all too near,
  And are trodden by careless feet.

VII.

But the flowers of the mountain bloom forme,
　Where no human foot hath trod,
And fresh and lovely they needs must be,
　That open so near to God.

VIII.

And onward she sped with her naked feet
　O'er the rough and stony road,
While the golden light of morn's early ray
　On the mountain summit glowed.

IX.

Annette, look down on your bleeding feet,
　You have reached the rocks on the brow,
None tread this path, save the wild goats fleet,--
　You may gather your garland now.

X.

The blossoms are blue and golden here,
　But they will not do for me,
My wreath must be twined of the flowers that none
　But God and His Angels see.

F

XI.

And she painfully climbs o'er the rocky way,

    But, alas! no flowers appear;

You had better go back, my poor Annette,

    You will find no garland here.

XII.

Yes, there is a flower all pure and white !

    See, it grows 'mid the thorns above !

I must gather that for the Christ Child bright,

    For purity wins His love.

XIII.

And over the rocks on the mountain top

    She is climbing on hands and feet,

And has gathered a flower like her child-like faith,

    As simple, and pure, and sweet.

XIV.

And here is another flower, Annette,

    Like the skies of the summer blue,

Emblem of Hope, by the good God sent

    For the Holy Child and you.

XV.

You have reached the top of the mountain now,
  But no more bright flowers appear,
The child looks on with a clouded brow,
  There are only brambles here.

XVI.

Yet stay, Annette; in the very midst
  Of the briers a blossom grows,
And its delicate bloom hath a colour faint
  As the tint of the palest rose.

XVII.

Her hands are pierced by the long sharp thorns,
  And the blood is flowing fast,
The pale pink flower is with crimson dyed,
  But the task is done at last.

XVIII.

But a sweet voice calls her; "O stop, Annette,
  Show those beautiful flowers to me,"
A lovely child on the rock is set,
  And he stays her pleadingly.

XIX.

Was it the light of the morning sun
    In his golden hair that played?
Or Annette's fancy, perchance, alone,
    That round him a glory made?

XX.

"Oh, give those flowers to me, Annette,"
    But the shepherd maiden smiled,
"I cannot give them to you," she said,
    "They are all for the Holy Child."

XXI.

"Give them to me, dear little Annette,"
    And the blue eyes eager grew,
"I will offer your flowers to the Holy Child,
    It will be the same to you."

XXII.

"And what shall I give Him, then, to-day,
    Ah no, dear little one, no,"
But the child in sorrow half turned away,
    And the tears began to flow.

XXIII.

" Nay, nay, dear little one, do not cry,

   Here take them,"—the infant smiled,

While the large drops stood in Annette's blue eye,

   "Take my flowers to the Holy Child."

XXIV.

And she gave him the flowers, but a bright tear fell.

   In the purple flower it lay—

If others to Jesus bring flowers, Annette,

   You have offered a gem to-day.

XXV.

The children have met in the village church,

   With their garlands fresh and sweet,

But no smile has the Holy Child bestowed

   On the treasures at His feet.

XXVI.

And little Annette is kneeling there,

   With her head bowed down in shame,

But a sweet low voice is speaking near,

   And it softly breathes her name.

XXVII.

"Oh, I cannot go to the Holy Child,"
 And her tears flow fast and free,
"I have no flowers for my Lord to-day,
 And he will not smile on me."

XXVIII.

Look up, look up, dear little Annette,
 What infant is standing there?
Is it the light of the morning sun
 That shines in his golden hair?

XXIX.

The child of the mountain, little Annette,
 Is the sweet Child Jesus, too;
He holds three flowers in His outstretched hand,
 And He only smiles on you—

XXX.

The lily of Faith, so pure and white,
 Hope's blossom of Heaven's own blue,
And Charity's flower with its diamond bright,
 And its rich deep crimson hue.

XXXI.

The flowers of the mountain little Annette,
   Whose pathway is rarely trod,
They won the smile of the Holy Child,
   They blossomed so near to God.

Restoration of Mayfield.

I.

Many a year, in lonely sadness,
  Have these silent ruins stood,
With no sound of Christian gladness
  Breaking on their solitude.
But our Lady well remembered,
  That the spot her own had been,
And the Angels knew that Mayfield
  Was once sacred to their Queen.

F*

II.

And the Saints have prayed for England,
   For the Island once their own,
Though error's gloomy mantle
   Hath round her long been thrown,
And by our God's great mercy
   They have not prayed in vain,
The Saint's old home at Mayfield,
   Is the Holy Child's again.

III.

Once again from aisle and chancel,
   Shall arise the Vesper hymn,
And the Ave bell at sunset
   Greet the twilight shadows dim.
Round the Virgin Mother's Altar
   Shall the faithful pray once more,
And the Church's children worship,
   Where their fathers knelt before.

IV.

And the patient, waiting Angels
   Who have charge from God, to keep

Watch and ward, o'er holy places,
  Where our sainted fathers sleep,
Once again shall raise their voices
  With our feeble tones, in prayer,
To the Sacred Heart of Jesus
  Throned, in hidden glory there.

V.

Now the loved ones gone before us,
  Will no more have cause to grieve
That the bell for the departed
  Tolls for prayers, in vain, at eve.
Many a loving "De Profundis,"
  Many a "May they rest in peace,"
Will the Angels bear to Jesus
  For His spouses quick release.

VI.

Surely Faith's clear day is dawning
  On the darkness of our night,
And the radiance of her morning
  Shall unclouded be, and bright;

Mary's star hath shone upon us,
  England's blessed Saints have prayed,
And God's mercy on His children,
  Will no longer be delayed.

The Seasons.

I.

I knew that I was called the Cross to bear,
And sad and weary down to rest I lay,
The earth was all so bright, so wondrous fair,
Why should I cast her proffered gifts away.

II.

At length I slept, and on a starry throne
I saw our Lady with the Holy Child;
My gentle Mother called me to her side,
While Jesus bade me stay, and sweetly smiled.

III.

And then I heard arise from Angel choirs
Sweet hyms to Jesus' and to Mary's Name,
While laden with fair gifts of fruit and flowers
To greet their Infant King, the Seasons came.

IV.

The first was Spring-tide; all her sunny hair
Sparkling with rain-drops as at Jesus' feet
She laid her gift, a wreath of early leaves
Twined with pale snowdrops and the violet sweet

V.

Then Jesus raised it, and "Henceforth," He said,
"My brightest blossoms, Spring, shall Mary claim
And while earth's children love their Virgin Queen
Thy fairest month shall bear her blessed Name."

VI.

Next, Summer came to worship, and she bore
Treasures to Jesus, from earth's brightest bowers,
Lilies and roses in the wreath she wore,
Were mingled with His own sad Passion flowers.

VII.

And Jesus blessed these flowers, "Evermore
Around my Altar throne, your place shall be,
Where Angels bright their hidden God adore,
Fair flowers," He said, " Ye shall abide with me."

VIII.

Then Autumn came, and kneeling, "Lord," she said
"Canst thou accept what is already thine ? "
And golden corn at Jesus' feet she laid,
Mixed with the purple clusters of the vine.

IX.

And Jesus spoke sweet comfort : "Blest are they
Who render back what is already Mine ;
Adored throughout all time thy God shall be,
Beneath the humble forms of bread and wine."

X.

Then last of all, came Winter, sad he stood,
His cheek bedewed with tears of love and grief,
His form was bowed beneath a Cross of wood,
And in his hand he held a thorny wreath.

XI.

He laid them down, and to the very ground
In shame and sorrow bent his agéd frame,
He dared not look at Jesus, but with tears
He faltered forth the Holy Child's sweet Name.

XII.

And Jesus smiled on winter, "Thou hast given
Of these fair gifts, the dearest and most blest,
Thy wreath of thorns shall crown the God of heaven,
Thy Cross of wood afford Him sweetest rest."

XIII.

"And is it thus dear Lord? and dost thou choose
For love of thankless man, a lot like this,
Earth's fairest, brightest gifts dost thou refuse
That thou may'st gain for me eternal bliss?

XIV.

"And shall I choose the flowers? O dearest Lord,
Which thou rejectest for the love of me!
No! let it be my hope, my sweet reward
To wear the thorns, and bear the Cross with thee."

A Dream.

I.

I dreamt that in our happy Convent home
We knelt, at evening, wrapt in silent prayer;
When lo! descending from His Altar throne,
Our Jesus came, and stood amongst us there.

II.

Then to each kneeling form methought He went,
Giving to each a smile, a loving word,
While in ecstatic joy each head was bent
To catch the whisper of our Infant Lord.

G

III.

Alas, it is but just, I sadly thought,
Since I so oft have turned sweet Lord from thee,
That thou, in angry silence, and with nought,
Not even a reproach, should'st turn from me.

IV.

Hot tears were streaming fast, when lo! I felt
Those tiny arms about my neck entwine,
And while enraptured and entranced I knelt,
The Holy Child's soft cheek was laid to mine.

V.

" And wherefore look so sad ?" He whispered low,
"Why are the bright tears streaming from thine eye
Though others may not heed thee, dear one! know
Thy little Brother could not pass thee by.

VI.

"Sorrow will come upon thee, thou mayest deem
Thy load of grief almost too great to bear,
But fear not then, though dark thy life may seem,
Thy little brother will be with thee there.

VII.

"And when life's ways are dreariest, when the cross
Hardest of all to bear, is laid on thee—
When those thou lovest have to suffer most,
Fear not for them, thy friends are dear to Me.

VIII.

" Grief cannot always last, life's close must come,
Then will I call thee from this desert wild,
Arise My well belov'd, My sister spouse,
Come dwell for ever with the Holy Child."

The Wolf of Gubbio.

Now all the men in Gubbio
  Have met in sad affright,
They cannot ply their work by day,
They cannot rest at night,
  Each mother clasps her infant
In terror, to her breast,
  And Gubbio's youths and maidens
Are pale and sore distressed.

II.

Within the waving forest,
  Upon yon hillside green,
A grisly wolf there lurketh,
  A savage beast I ween!
Full many a gallant hunter
  Hath sought his lair in vain,
For all came disappointed
  To Gubbio back again.

III.

Woe to the wretched mother
  Who leaves her child asleep!
Woe to the careless herdsman
  Who doth not guard his sheep!
The empty cradle standeth
  Besmeared with crimson gore,
And of the flock the finest
  And fairest are no more.

IV.

The townsmen met in council
  In the broad market place,

And every heart was heavy,

And pale was every face,

When lo ! there stood among them

In hood and habit brown,

The holy Brother Francis

Who came to bless their town.

V.

Around the Saint they gathered,

And told their cause of grief,

And straight he said, "My children,

Our Lord will send relief,

For aid he ne'er refuseth

To those who humbly pray,

And now to yonder mountain

Take ye with me the way."

VI.

They formed a long procession ;

Old men bowed down and gray,

The young men from the vine-yards,

The children from their play,

And when they reached the mountain,
  Straightway before them all
Did holy Brother Francis
  Upon the wild beast call.

VII.

And lo! behold a wonder!
  All down the mountain green
In peaceful fashion coming,
  The savage beast was seen.
Women shrank back affrighted,
  Old men stood still amazed,
And all on Brother Francis
  In awe-struck wonder gazed.

VIII.

But when the wolf had reached them,
  The restless beast stood still,
And looked at Brother Francis
  As though to learn his will:
And thus the Saint spoke gently,
  "My brother, wolf I fear

Thou little know'st the havoc

   Thou hast been making here.

IX.

"These Christians good regard thee

   With terror and dismay,

Thou hast devoured their children,

   And driven their flocks away,

But deem not little brother,

   That thou hast blame from me,

In all thou hast but acted

   As God has given to thee.

X.

"Yet now I must forbid thee,

   To do us further harm,

Or cause the men of Gubbio

   To live in dire alarm.

Henceforward thou shalt leave us

   Good wolf, from terror free,

Whilst we, oh shaggy brother

   Will feed thee, faithfully."

G*

XI.

He sent them for some brown bread,
And share of last year's corn,
While some looked on in wonder,
And some looked on in scorn.
But when they saw the wild beast
Eat from the good Saint's hand,
A murmur of thanksgiving
Rose up from all the band.

XII.

Once more spoke Brother Francis.
"Good brother part we now,
As Gubbio's men are faithful,
So, faithful too be thou.
Hold'st thou to our agreement?
Then, this thy pledge shall be,
Before all these good people,
Give thou, thy paw to me."

XIII.

Behold! on three legs only,
The beast contrived to stand,

And laid his shaggy fore-paw
  Within the good Saint's hand.
Such power from God doth ever
  The pure of heart possess
Over the savage natures,
  That roam the wilderness.

XIV.

For food each day, at noon-tide,
  Thenceforth the creature came,
The people, when they saw him
  Would bless God's Holy Name.
At last upon the hill-side
  They found his portion left,
All Gubbio mourned in sorrow,
  As of a friend bereft.

XV.

Still mothers to their children
  The wondrous story tell,
Of what upon that hill-side
  In ancient times befel.

Still pray they to St. Francis,

That as from every ill,

Of old, he freed their good town,

He may preserve it still.

The Wooden Candlestick.

I.

It was a Convent poor and lone,

That stood for many a year

In honour of our Lady's Name,

Groningen's city near.

II.

No stately church the convent owned,

Its chapel was of wood,

Plain as the poorest peasant's hut,

The little building stood.

III.

But one rich jewel it possessed,
  And well the nuns might hold
The treasure which their temple graced
  More dear than gems or gold.

IV.

It was an image of their Queen,
  With her sweet Child divine,
Won by Crusaders long ago
  In holy Palestine.

V.

The beauty of that Mother's face,
  ('Twas thus the legend ran,)
Its sweetness and its matchless grace
  Were not the work of man.

VI.

'Twas said that none but Angels bright
  Who had our Lady seen,
Could e'er have carved so wond'rous fair
  An image of their Queen.

VII.

Once when "Et Homo factus est,"
   On Mary's Feast was said,
The Holy Child His crown had placed
   Upon our Lady's head.

VIII.

And from that time since He had made
   His will so clearly known,
The simple wreath of flowers was worn
   By Mary, Queen alone.

IX.

And now the glorious Feast came round,
   The brightest of the year,
The day on which her Jesus crowned
   His Virgin Mother dear.

X.

Two fair wax candles decked the shrine
   And garlands of bright flowers,
But dark the poor brass lamp must be
   Through all the silent hours.

XI.

Alas! the Sisters had no oil;
  But while they knelt in prayer
A wooden candlestick they placed
  And tall wax taper there.

XII.

They could not leave it thro' the night,
  The taper would burn low,
And sadly do they quench the light
  Ere from the church they go.

XIII.

But thro' the chapel windows lo!
  A shining light they see!
The taper by our Lady's shrine
  Is burning brilliantly.

XIV.

Again they quench it but again,
  The light shines bright and clear;
And now they kneel around her shrine,
  And bless our Lady dear.

XV.

The good priest bade them leave it there,
  "We may be sure," said he,
"Aught that our Lady hath in care,
  Guarded right well must be."

XVI.

And all the year, the legend tells,
  That wond'rous taper burned,
And grew no less, till once again,
  Our Lady's Feast returned.

XVII.

Then was their oil cask filled once more;
  And Mary's taper dear,
Their blessed Mother's gift was kept
  And treasured many a year.

The Marigold.

I.

Long years ago, ere faith and love
  Had left our land to sin and shame,
Her children called my blossoms bright
By their sweet Mother's gentle name.
And when amid the leaflets green
  They saw sweet "Mary buds" unfold,
In honour of the angel's Queen
  They plucked the royal Marigold.

II.

I was the favorite of the poor,
  And bloomed by every cottage door,
Speaking of heaven's fair Queen to men;
  They loved me for the name I bore.
There is no love for Mary now,
  And Faith died out when love grew cold;
Men seldom raise their hearts to heaven
  Through looking at the Marigold.

III.

But Mary from her throne on high
  Still looks on England and on me,
The name-sake of the Queen am I,
  The Lady of the land is She.
And surely She must win once more
  Her heritage to Christ's true fold;
Then to Her children, as of yore
  Will preach again the Marigold.

Legend of the Mimulus.

I.

When 'neath the aged olive trees

  My Lord lay prostrate on the ground,

And bore his awful agony,

  Men say my blossoms grew around;

And when from out His sacred pores

  The crimson drops in anguish rolled,

Drawn by the crimes of sinful men,

  They fell upon my robe of gold.

II.

Since that dread hour, as earth's vain sons
   Their prince's favours proudly wear,
Those tokens of earth's sinless One
   Do I, upon my petals bear.
And simple souls who loved to trace
   The memory of their Lord, in me,
Have blessed me for those crimson stains,
   And called my name Gethsemane.

Prophecy of St. Ignatius.

He rode at the head of a gorgeous train,

Through the sun-lit hills of his own bright Spain;

His heart was joyous, his hopes were high,

For life seemed fair as the summer sky;

And ambition was there, he would noblest be

Mid his native land's proud Chivalry.

Crowds paused to gaze at the boyish grace

The last fair son of his haughty race,

The last of a line that had stained its name

With the foulest crimes, and the darkest shame.

But they looked on that forehead so broad and fair,
No trace of crime, or of shame was there;
But the ardent flush of a spirit gay
In the first bright dawn of life's early day.

A mendicant stood in the crowded way,
As the prince rode by on that festal day;
A mendicant weary, and poor, and lame,
None knew his errand, none asked his name,
But they frowned on the stranger : Why stood he there
To mar with his presence a scene so fair?

His cheek was pale, but his smile was bright,
And his dark eyes glowed with a mystic light,
As he smiled on the noble, princely boy,
His fair face beaming with hope and joy :
"The opening blossom," he said," I see,
But oh far other the fruit will be."

"I thank thee, Lord, for this precious gem,
It will show so fair in thy diadem."
The people scoffed, as he murmured low,—
"Madmen or fools would but whisper so, "
But that mendicant saw into future years—
With their joys and sorrows, their smiles and tears ;
For the fire that glowed in his deep dark eye,
Had been lit by the spirit of prophecy.

Years have rolled on, and that boy's proud name

Is a household word in the homes of Spain ;

He had dreamed of honours in field and hall,

Of wealth and power, he had won them all ;

Yet his heart was sad when he knelt in prayer,

For the mendicant's blessing was working there.

Again did the prince and the beggar meet,

But not as then, in the crowded street ;

No throngs are shouting with loud acclaim

Through the squares of the city De Borgia's name,

No neighing charger with trappings bright,

Bears the noble form of the Spanish Knight,

He wears no helmet, no jewelled sword,

And serves no king, but his suffering Lord.

He has left the court, with its pomp and pride,

That poor lame beggar his help and guide ;

At the pilgrim's feet he hath cast him down,

He prays to be clad in the coarse grey gown,

And banished for aye are the dreams of youth,

In the strong bright light of God's radiant truth

A wondrous triumph His grace hath won

In that glorious sire, and his saintly son.

H*

A Legend of Japan.

It was a distant eastern land, where in the sun's clear
   light

The Ximo's smiling valleys lay in tranquil beauty
   bright;

And there a stately palace rose, and hills and for-
   ests green,

Where glittering streams sweet music made, to grace
   that lovely scene.

The sounds of laughter soft and low, and joyous
   voices rose

In happy murmurs 'neath its walls, at morn' and
   evening's close,

And graceful forms as fair and bright as were its
  own sweet flowers

Glided like things of life and light amid its sunny
  bowers.

The very pathway flashed and gleamed in the red
  sunset ray,

As though rich gems of every hue beset the jewelled way.

The brilliant plumage of strange birds glance
  'twixt the blossoms rare;

All glorious things of earth and sea were brought
  and garnered there.

A fairy temple had been raised in which might
  dwell apart

The creature at whose feet was laid the worship
  of a heart.

And she,—the idol of that shrine,—the treasure
  held so dear

That foot of man might scarce approach its gorgeous casket near;

But that she breathed, she might have seemed a
  form of marble cold,

A statue in a fairy scene, mid flashing gems and
  gold.

The smile, that wreathed her pallid lip was like
the sun-light shed

In mockery, by noon's golden ray, upon the silent
dead.—

They wooed her with a thousand wiles—they brought
the young and gay,

They strove to win her into smiles with dance
and joyous lay.—

And when they saw the pale stern grief in that
sad woman's face,

They marvelled how, mid joys like hers, sorrow
ceuld hold its place.

Oh little knew they of the woe, that hath its
secret springs,

Where life's dark silent waters flow amid earth's
brightest things.

They knew not how her soul had yearned through
the dull weary years,

With a longing all too strong for words—a grief
too deep for tears.

They saw not at her side a form which she
could ever see,

The sight that gave those dark bright eyes their
look of misery.

They heard not in each gust of wind an infant's
wailing cry,

Nor saw its robe in each bright cloud, the summer breeze bore by,

But they noted that a child's low sob brought
to the marble cheek

A hectic flush, that told the pang her voice
refused to speak.

And in the palace garden now at the soft evening hour

She sat beneath the waving plants, within a rosy
bower ;

Her maidens sang their gayest song, and told their
blithest tale,

Striving in vain with arts, that yet they knew too
well must fail.

But there was one in that gay band, who gazed
with tearful eye

Upon the sad and gentle queen, who sighed so
wearily.

Unlike she was to all the rest, though courtly
robes she wore,

Was it because upon her breast a little cross she
bore ?

To her they turned in thoughtless mood, "oh tell
us gentle Grace,

Why every sunrise sees you seek each weird and
lonely place?"

"They say that in the fresh cool hours the dew
hath virtues rare,

And opening buds have wondrous power for keep-
ing maidens fair ;

But stranger tales than these we hear—that not
for blossoms bright,

Nor pearly dew, do you arise before the morning
light."

"They say—oh! Lady, can it be—that you but
seek to save

Babes, by their parents cast away, from an untimely
grave.

"That in your mantle softly wrapped each wretched
child you bear

To where the black-robed bonzes dwell—the Christian
men of prayer."

"That Ucondono's daughter fair—the favourite of
our queen,

Washing those infants in the stream, has many a
time been seen."

In mirthful, mocking tones, they spoke, but oh!
an idle word

Hath many a time, unwitting, broke some aching
heart that heard.

Now the wan cheek of that sad queen grew strangely,
wildly bright,

And from the depths of her dark eyes flashed an
unearthly light,

With lips that moved, yet made no sound, and
outstretched hands she gazed

On the young Christian, while around her maidens
sat amazed.

Then, smiling on the spell-bound queen, the fair
girl gently spoke,

Like music rung from harps unseen, her voice the
stillness broke;

"Nay, no dishonour can befal my brave and
noble sire

By any act God's holy law may from his child
require;

The proudest in our haughty land might gladly
stoop to save

The precious souls, for whom that God His sole
Begotten gave.

Oh you would join me in the work, if but that
    cost ye knew,

And count it as the noblest deed a woman's hand
    may do.

Then in a whisper, "oh sweet queen might I of
    Jesus teach,

How gently would He heal the wound, no other
    hand may reach!

In the dear order of His love all trouble worketh
    good,

And sorrow hath a special grace—its own Beati-
    tude."—

The tears through hopeless years unshed, from their
    sealed fountains gushed,

That fragile form shook with the sobs, that had
    so long been hushed,

"Oh Grace," the words broke forth at last, "you
    have done this—and I,—

"I let them doom my loved—my own—my royal
    babe to die!

For one short hour, within my arms I held him
    on my breast,

And then, despite his mother's cries, they tore
    him from his rest.

I

They said, that in a monarch's son no blemish
    must they find,

And he my first, my only one, oh Grace my boy
    was blind.

Talk not to me of God's dear love! Maiden! love
    had no part

In sending that sweet face to mock a woman's
    bleeding heart!

One long, long kiss, and then they tore my life's
    dear light away!

All hope, all trust, all faith in heaven died in my
    soul that day.

Grace I have never wept till now,—I told my
    grief to none;

But my spirit's depths were stirred to-day when
    they said what you had done.

And I must be a Christain Grace! oh teach your
    faith to me!

Yours is a God of pitying love,—His servant I
    would be."—

A golden glory seemed to rest on Grace's upturned
    brow,

As she murmured, 'mid her happy tears, "My God
    I thank thee now:

I thank Thee for this noble soul through fiery
trouble won,

Oh perfect I beseech Thee Lord, the work so well
begun."

And then the young Apostle rose, and held the
Cross on high,

While she told them of the Christian's God—the
Lord of earth and sky.

And of the mighty love, that drew the Eternal
from His throne

To dwell among the sons of earth, a stranger 'mid
His own,—

But when she spoke of Bethlehem's cave and of
the mother maid,

Of the manger, and the hard rough straw whereon
the Child was laid;

And then of Mary's tender love for our unhappy
race

A smile of mingled hope and peace lit up the
queen's sad face.

"O if all broken hearts," she said, "have thus a
claim on thee,

Mother, before thy Son on high, thou wilt remem-
ber me."

All through the long dim corridors, in silence to
and fro

Slight, dusky forms were flitting past with footfall
hushed and low.

It was the lonely midnight hour and in a gorgeous
room

Lighted by one pale lamp, and gems that sparkled
in the gloom,

Arima's queen, in snow-white robes, was kneeling,
wrapt in prayer

Amid the youthful Christian band, that gathered
round her there.

Strange was the picture they beheld, who saw the
midnight scene,

The shadowy forms, the regal hall, and that fair
kneeling queen.

The same young graceful girls were there, who in
the Summer's pride

Had met beneath the garden trees in the calm
even-tide

Then, joyous as the bright-winged birds they flutter-
ed 'mid the flowers,

Like the gay fire-flies of their land through all
life's sunny hours.

While one alone of all their band like marble statue
cold

Among them moved, and scarcely seemed a thing
of earthly mould.

Yet she, where all were young and fair, the loveliest,
aye, had been—

Most richly gifted,—most beloved,—the saddest,—and
a queen.

Now all was changed,—mute forms they stood, whose
tones had music made

The glowing cheeks had paled like flowers, that all
too early fade.

And when, upon the listening ear fell some chance
midnight sound

Each lip was blanched, as though with fear, each
trembling glanced around.

While she alone, for whom they feared, was kneeling radiant there

With sparkling drops of crystal sheen upon her
raven hair.

The young Apostle near her stood,—her mission
ended now,

Her hand the saving stream had poured upon the
queen's fair brow,

And, as it fell, the maiden's vow was registered
    above—

The minister of God's dear grace should own no earthly
    love.

Sweet Jesus was it ever known, or can it ever be,

That man's poor gifts were not repaid a thousand-fold
    by Thee?

Hath weeping suppliant ever knelt at blessed Mary's
    feet,

And come away with heart unsoothed by heavenly
    comfort sweet?

Into the mother's spirit came that night a strange deep
    joy,

She knew that Jesus in His love had saved her sightless
    boy.

No angel whisper smote her ear—in her glad heart
    alone

She felt, that she should meet her child before the great
    White Throne,

And could this be? At that same hour in Nangazaki
    fair

Lay wrapped in childhood's slumber sweet, Arima's
    infant heir;

And blind no more—they who had saved with loving
  tears implored

That for their father Francis' sake his sight might be
  restored.

And now within the college walls he dwelt in careless
  glee

Oft dreaming of the mother dear, whom he in Heaven
  might see.

And might that mother never clasp her long lost darling
  here,

Nor hear the voice, that would have made such music in
  her ear ?

Yes once she saw him—when dark clouds had gathered
  o'er the land,

And persecution's flaming sword waved in her blood-red
  hand.

They brought him to her, when she sat at the still
  sunset hour,

As on that eventide long past, beneath the garden
  bower;

The mother's cheek grew deadly pale, as once again she
  pressed

The treasure, lost through those long years, upon her
  aching breast.

While he, unwitting, marvelled much what made the
    Lady weep;

He loved her—she had often come to see him in his
    sleep—

He spoke in artless childish way, and God alone
    could see

How the bleeding heart, beneath his words, quivered in
    agony—

One wild bright gleam flashed as of old from out the
    clear dark eye;

And then she kissed the boy's fair brow, and gave him
    back—to die.—

She turned away, and passed once more into her stately
    home,

Those regal halls to which for her earth's joys might
    never come.—

And wearily the years went by, while all around
    her fell

The young, the beautiful, the bright—friends loved so
    long and well.

She saw them win the martyr's crown, and still her
    prayer must be

" When wilt Thou hear my cry, O Lord—when shall I
    come to Thee"?—

Her faith was known—but who might dare to touch
the charmed life

Of that long loved—long worshipped one—Fondoso-
dono's wife?

O human love! oh human heart, unhallowed by God's
grace?

Say who would wish within thy shrine to win the highest
place?

It was his voice that spoke at last the treasured idol's
doom,

His very love that laid his queen within her early
tomb.

Defeated—conquered—now were his the palace halls
alone—-

But she should die as she had lived—his only—all his
own.

Her maidens wept that their sweet queen no martyr's
crown might wear,

Fain had they seen her in the church the glorious palm
branch bear

They wondered too, who saw her die, at her calm
steadfast mien,

And thought perchance some stern reproach for him
there should have been

1*

They knew not, that to her sad heart, death could bring
    nought but joy,
Since 'neath the gorgeous plane trees' shade she kissed
    her martyr boy,
They knew not that her glorious crown, was like our
    Lady's won,
When with the lance upon the cross they pierced her
    only son.

Some years after the death of St. Francis Xavier, the Queen of Tango was converted to Christianity through the teaching of one of her ladies, the daughter of a Christian noble. The king who was passionately attached to her, seldom permitted her to quit the precincts of the palace, and never allowed her to go out unattended by spies of his own. Under these circumstances it became impossible for Father Organtin, a Jesuit missionary residing in Tango, to procure access to the queen, in order to administer the Sacrament of Baptism, which she therefore received from the hands of the young girl by whom she had been instructed. The king soon became aware of the change in her religion, but as a fiery persecution of the Christians had just broken out, his love for her induced him to conceal the fact. Shortly afterwards, being about to undertake an expedition against the neighbouring states, he resolved that in case of his death, his queen should not survive him, and he gave orders to that effect to the officer whom he left in charge of his palace. In the war that ensued, the king was taken prisoner, and the officer put the queen to death, in compliance with the wishes of his sovereign.

On these historical incidents Lady G. Fullerton has founded the touching story of the Queen of Arima and her martyr boy, so beautifully told in "Laurentia."

The Lord of Crequy.

I.

The Baron of Crequy's brow was sad
 For his heart was full of woe,
And he paced 'neath the oaks in the woodland glade
 With a heavy step and slow.
He held a Cross in his mailèd hand,
 But the baron did not pray,
He muttered in thoughtful tone and low
 (What will my Lady say?)

II.

Oh what will she say, and what will she do
My beautiful summer bride !
Will she deem that a loyal knight and true
Thus early should leave her side?
Yet I may not linger in silken bower
When the Oriflamme floats free
And God's dear honour is sore assailed
By the might of Paynimrie.

III.

The Baron entered the lordly bower
Where his Lady sat alone,
Her head bowed low like a drooping flower
When the Light of the Sun is gone.
"Now droop not thus my lily bright,
Look up fair Lady mine,
And pray God speed thine own true knight
To the land of Palestine."

IV.

"God speed thee then my own true knight"
Alas ! for my foolish fears,

I know men cannot endure the sight

    Of a woman's flowing tears.

But my own brave Raoul to linger here

.   Were shame to thy knighthood's pride,

It must never be said that a Lady's tears

    Detained thee at her side.

V.

" The Baron hath taken her wedding ring

    And he snapped the gold in twain,

I trust in honour to come, he said,

    When I bring thee this again ;

Yet in search of fame sweet Lady mine

    I do not cross the sea,

But to fight for my Lord in Palestine

    Where he lived and died for me."

VI.

The oars are loosed, and the sails unfurled,

    The fleet speeds on its way,

But a messenger followed in haste from France

    To fair Satalia's bay'

To the Sire de Crequy the courier came
  "Good tidings" he said "I bear,
With a greeting kind from thy noble dame
  Lord Baron thou hast an heir."

VII.

"Now God be thanked, To my Lady bright
  Good Squire speed thou from me,
Bid her have no fear for her own true knight
  I am going to victory."
Oh ! little he deemed that warrior bold
  That the passions of Christian men
Were a surer defence to the Paynim hold
  Than the swords of the Saracen.

VIII.

The hosts have landed on Palestine's strand,
  And each noble heart beat high,
They would fight for their Lord in the Holy Land
  They would win in His cause or die.
And they eagerly looked for the Christian bands
  Who should gladly greet them there,

But nought they saw save the golden sands,
　And the summer cloudlets fair.

IX.

Fair France's monarch and Hungary's king
　May strive for awhile in vain,
Ere weary hearted they sadly turn
　To that bright blue sea again.
For busied with feudal jars are they
　Who would rule where Jesus died,
And Christian men are his fiercest foes
　In their sinful wrath and pride.

X.

One short year passed and they stood once more,
　The last of that glorious band,
On the sunny sands of that Eastern shore,
　They were leaving the Holy Land.
But each gauntleted hand was fiercely clenched,
　There were frowns on each stern brow,
And the words they murmured too plainly told
　They were foes to their brethren now.

XI.

The nobles of Europe in grief and ire
　　Right well from that land may part
As they think of St. Bernard's words of fire
　　And a Pontiff's broken heart.
And the Baron of Crequy—where was he?
　　In a Saracen dungeon deep;
But they deemed him dead in his own countrie
　　And they bore the news to his sad Ladye;
Oh what could she do but weep?

XII.

Slowly and sadly the days crept on;
　　They brought him a caftan green,
And proffered a turban sparkling bright
　　With ruby and emerald sheen.
But brighter still was the angry gleam
　　In the Baron's flashing eye,
"Hath the infidel Soldan now to learn
　　That a Christian knight can die"!

XIII.

Ah! death perchance were an easy thing;
　　But not in those chains to lie,

For a free bold spirit that longed to gaze
  On the clear blue summer sky.
The raven hair was with silver streaked,
  And the flashing eye grew dim,
And the days that passed in that dungeon lone
  Were as months, aye years, to him.

XIV.

And to years they lengthened, and still he lay
  In the Saracen chieftain's hold,
Till they came to his prison one summer day
  And his final doom was told.
"As a Saracen Emir, O Christian brave
  Come forth on the green earth free,
Or find in this dungeon thy nameless grave,
  To-morrow thy choice must be."

XV.

One thought he gave to his sad Ladye,
  One thought to his infant son,
But on scimiter keen or on caftan green
  He wasted, I ween, not one.

K

But he bent his knee to our dear Ladye,

    And he clasped his hands in prayer,

And into his soul sweet slumber stole

    As he knelt in silence there.

XVI.

Oh not in a Syrian dungeon deep

    Lay the Baron when he woke,

But the song of the birds in his own dear land

    On his spell-bound senses broke.

The breeze of the morning wandered by

    And lifted his tangled hair,

And surely never 'neath Eastern Sky

    Floated clouds so fleecy and fair.

XVII.

Was it a dream that over him waved

    The old oak branches green,

That the tall brown ferns on his fevered brow

    Shed the glittering dewdrops sheen.

That the fragrance faint of all woodland flowers

    Like a message from home came by

Or had he but dreamed of those captive years

   In the land of Paynimrie.

XVIII.

A shepherd stood at the Baron's side,

   And no Syrian garb he wore,

But an image of Jesus Crucified

   On his stalwart breast he bore.

And he spoke in the dear Provençal tongue

   "Now speak by the Holy Rood!

What bringeth thee here in thy garments weird

   And thy chains, to Crequy wood?"

XIX.

What brought him there? But a short hour since

   In the Syrian hold he lay,

And now he stood in his own dear land,

   In the light of God's bright day.

But when was it known that Mary's love

   Failed her children in their need?

Our Lady's hand from the Paynim Land

   Had her faithful servant freed.

XX.

No word in answer the Baron spoke
　　But he dropped upon his knee,
He thought of his prayer to our Lady dear,
　　And he knew that he was free.
And when he arose "Lead on" he said,
　　"To the Lady of Crequy's bower,
I am come as one from the silent dead
　　For this is our Lady's hour."

XXI.

The shepherd glanced at the Baron's weeds,
　　And he laughed aloud in scorn,
"'Twere well such a guest as thou to lead
　　To our dame on her bridal morn !
Her bridal morn—though in sooth it seems
　　A bridal sad to be,
Yet, trust me friend, they will scarcely find
　　A welcome there for thee."

XXII.

The Baron in silence turned away;
　　Oh would it indeed be so !

And he thought of another bridal day,

  In the bright years long ago.

And tears gushed forth from the strong man's eyes

  As with rapid step he strode;

And took his stand were the twain must pass

  On the old familiar road.

XXIII.

Oh! little they thought who saw him there

  Mid the wondering peasant crowd,

That the haggard man with the unkempt hair

  Was the Baron of Crequy proud.

They carelessly told of the Lady's woe

  Since the death of her noble knight,

How the Baron's brother had proved her foe,

  And had robbed her of her right.

XXIV.

And how Sir Raoul's most trusty friend

  At last had the Lady won,

Though she wedded only the gossips said

  For the sake of her infant son.

They came—and the Baron's gaze was bent
 On the fair face of the bride,
And he knew the stately warrior tall
 Who was riding at her side.

XXV.

But her graceful head was in sadness bowed,
 Her blue eyes dimmed with tears,
Could this be the bride so trusting and proud
 He had wedded in by-gone years?
He stepped from the crowd by the roadside there
 And he bent to earth his knee,
"I bring thee a token, O Lady fair,
 From the Land of Paynimrie."

XXVI.

He drew from the breast of his tattered vest
 The broken wedding ring;
To see the flush on the Lady's cheek
 I ween was a gladsome thing.
The old light shone in the clear blue eye
 As she spoke right eagerly,

"The Baron of Crequy a token gave

   When he took that ring from me."

XXVII.

"Sir Raoul answered" the Baron said

   As he snapped the gold in twain,

"I hope in honour to come to thee

   When I bring thee this again.

Yet in search of fame sweet Lady mine

   I do not cross the Sea

But to fight for my Lord in Palestine

   Where He lived and died for me."

XXVIII.

"And there have I borne these ten long years

   The captive's galling chain

But our Lady's grace hath brought me here

   To mine own dear land again."

No word the gentle Lady spake

   Though her face was lit with joy

But she led a child to her kneeling lord

   And bade him bless his boy.

XXIX.

There was feasting high in de Crequy's halls

And joyous hearts that day,

When the Baron sat mid his noble guests

With his gentle Lady gay.

He rose and lifted his plumed cap

While he spoke right reverently,

"Now God be thanked for his mighty love

And blest be our dear Ladye."

"Taken from the Legends of Our Lady. No alteration has been made in the story with the exception of the omission of some minor details, and an illusion made through inadvertence to Provence, whereas the domain of Crequy is stated in the Legends of our Lady to have been situated in Brittany. A still more extraordinary legend is said to be familiar to the Breton people, who relate that the Lord of Gars and his esquire having been taken prisoners by the Saracens, were shut up by their captors in a large box, which they were about to bury in the earth when the Baron commended himself to our Lady vowing to erect a chapel in her honour if he should escape. Immediately they felt the box in motion, and confident that the Mother of God had heard the Baron's prayer. In fact the chest was found by some peasants on the road to Gars who liberated the prisoners in whom they recognised with astonishment their Lord and his esquire. The Baron fulfilled his vow by erecting a beautiful Gothic Chapel to our Lady of Bethlehem, which is still standing, and contains an old stained glass window representing the escape of the two captives and their transmission to Brittany."

The Lily.

I.

A maiden said to a Lily

  "I go to the dance to-night,

Wilt thou nestle among my tresses

  O Lily so pure and white?"

But the Lily answered: "O maiden,

  I should droop in the heat and glare,

And die in thy shining ringlets,

  Place the glowing carnation there."

K·

II.

A bride saw the Lily blooming,

"I go to the Altar to-day ;

In my bridal garland, sweet Lily

I will twine thy pale beautiful spray."

"Why sadden thy bridal, Lady

By wearing my cold white flowers?

Sweet roses and orange blossoms

Should gladden thy joyous hours."

III.

A mother wept o'er the lily ;

" In thy pallid beauty rare

Thou shalt lie on my dead child's bosom,

For surely thy place is there."

"O mourning, sorrowful mother,

Thou hast seen one blossom fade ;

On the shroud of thy broken lily,

Be a wreath of immortelles laid."

IV.

A young girl whispered : "O Lily,

Let me place thee on my breast,

For the sweet Lord Jesus cometh

   To-day in my heart to rest."

And the Lily murmured : "Yes maiden,

   On thy heart let my blossoms lie,

That my pure white petals may wither

   Near the Lord of purity."

Y.B.S.

A Legend of the Rosary.

I.

In the bright land of fair Provence,
    A lowly orphan dwelt,
And day by day at Mary's shrine
    The little maiden knelt.

II.

No watchful mother's tender care
    The child had ever known;
And so, the simple peasant folk
    Had called her Mary's own.

III.

For orphans ever, so they said
  To Mary's care are given;
And children all of parents dead
  Have twofold claim on heaven.

IV.

And as among the woods and fields,
  The little orphan grew;
The old Church windows' storied panes
  Were all the books she knew.

V.

And surely for Our Lady's child
  No better books could be;
For of her mother's life they showed
  Each wondrous mystery.

VI.

And never passed a day whate'er
  The orphan's task might be,
But at Our Lady's feet she knelt,
  To say the Rosary.

VII.

But once it chanced, that wearied out,
   She sought her humble bed;
Forgetting quite that she had left
   Her Rosary unsaid.

VIII.

When lo! within her little room
   She saw a wondrous light;
While floated round a sweet perfume,
   From countless roses bright.

IX.

And by her bed a Lady stood,
   The orphan knew her well,
And from her royal mantle's folds,
   That wondrous fragrance fell.

X.

She knew her by the twelve bright stars
   The radiant brow that crowned;
And by the mantle azure blue,
   With fairest roses bound.

XI.

The child kneels down while love and awe
    Her wondering spirit fill;
When lo! upon Our Lady's robe,
    A rose is wanting still.

XII.

And softly, sweetly, Mary spoke:
    "My child, these roses see
The fragrant wreath thy love hath twined
    From day to day for me."

XIII.

"But wherefore, hast thou left undone
    Thy work of love to-day?
How comes it that thou hast forgot
    My Rosary to say?"

XIV.

"So many on the great wide earth
    . Forget their Lord and me
And bring no flower,—but surely thou
    Wilt not unfaithful be!"

XV.

The little child has bowed her head
In shame her breast upon :
And now that vision heavenly bright
Has vanished and is gone.

XVI.

With tears the Rosary is said ;
But ever from that day,
The child drooped slowly like a flower
That fades from earth away.

XVII.

As though she could not linger here,
To whom it had been given
To see Our gentle Lady dear,
In that brief glimpse of heaven.

XVIII.

And Pilgrims to Our Lady's shrine
Would often go to see
Her grave, whom Mary's self had taught
To say the Rosary.

The Golden Ciborium.

(From the French.)

I.

My story is of that dread time,
　　When wicked men with fire and sword,
Strove to destroy the Church of God,
　　And madly raved against their Lord.

II.

A Holy priest, their fury feared,
　　And in a vase of crystal bright
He trembling placed the Sacred Host,
　　And hid it out of all men's sight.

L*

III.

The little vase with care he sealed,

And buried it within the earth,

Which surely ne'er before had held

A treasure of such priceless worth.

IV.

And then with many a tear and prayer

He sadly went upon his way,

Commending to God's holy care

The spot wherein his treasure lay.

V.

The danger passed and he returned,

When lo, a wonder! for behold!

The little crystal vase, is now

A rich ciborium of bright gold.

VI.

No allegory, dearest child,

Is this true story I have told,

And much I love this little tale

Of the ciborium turned to gold.

VII.

Your little heart, must be a vase
    Of clearest crystal, pure and bright,
When from His throne in Heaven above
    Comes down to you the Lord of Light.

VIII.

No taint of sin, no earthly stain,
    The brightness of that vase must dim;
Keep it, like Mary's spotless heart,
    Holy and pure, and free for him.

IX.

My own dear Lord if thou wilt deign,
    Within my little heart to come,
I'll strive, with all my feeble strength
    To purify thy lowly home.

X.

Thine own ciborium it shall be,
    Alas! not rich with gems or gold;
Wilt thou not bring, sweet Lord, to me
    What most thou lovest to behold?

XI.

Sweet meekness and humility,

　With charity's bright burning fire,

Patience, and gentle modesty,—

　Behold the gold which I desire.

XII

But then my child, the little vase,

　Made no resistance to my power ;

Say, will it be, the same with thee

　In thy sweet first Communion hour ?

XIII.

Ah yes, dear Lord ; with thy sweet grace,

　Faithful henceforth thy child will be ;

Nor ever lose or dim the gold

　With which thy love has gifted me.